THE SHAPE OF EVERY MONSTER YET TO COME

Brian Allen Carr

Lazy Fascist Press
PO Box 10065
Portland, OR 97296

www.lazyfascistpress.com
lazyfascist@gmail.com

ISBN: 978-1-62105-166-4

Cover Design by Matthew Revert
www.matthewrevert.com

Edited by Cameron Pierce

Printed in the USA.

PRAISE FOR BRIAN ALLEN CARR'S
THE LAST HORROR NOVEL IN THE
HISTORY OF THE WORLD

"Carr's magic shows in how he handles territory most would strand as genre. He fills the pages with magnetic, mostly sparse language, not far from how Robert Coover's recreations bring new threads to a corpse. His new mythology, set right in the middle of nowhere that many would consider the heartland of our country, is new and old at once, sick and rhapsodic, alive and not afraid to die."

—VICE

"From the same mind that brought you the delightfully subversive *Motherfucking Sharks* comes this cataclysmic novella, which explores how a ragtag group in Scrape, Texas, deals with unnatural and supernatural phenomena, drawing on elements of Mexican folklore, the insularity of small-town life, and the machinations of bodiless hands."

—BARNES & NOBLE BOOK BLOG

"Brian Allen Carr's *The Last Horror Novel in the History of the World* is a bewildering book—a work of low-key madness."

—HTML GIANT

"[L]augh-out-loud funny and relentlessly, shockingly grim."

—FANGORIA

"The book is a volatile mix of humor and horror, cementing itself as one of the best books of 2014."

—THE ARKHAM DIGEST

TABLE OF CONTENTS

THE SHAPE OF EVERY MONSTER YET TO COME

STAMP #3

Once, my mother sent me into the backyard to fetch a stick she intended to swat me with.

"Don't get a weak one neither," she said, "you make sure it's stiff enough to draw blood."

I slipped sad lipped from the back porch, my eyes wet with fear, and I scurried through the yard breaking all the twigs and fallen branches I could find, making them too tiny to swing.

Then, the oddest thing: I saw a magnolia flower in full bloom, its white petals opened up like silky tongues. I plucked it and ran it inside.

My mother was at the kitchen table smoking a Pall Mall, the ash on it long as a child's pinky finger.

I set the flower on the table in front of her, the place a plate would go if she were eating.

"What's this?" she asked.

"I couldn't find a good stick," I told her.

She took a drag off her cigarette, ashed above the flower—the charred bits of tobacco and paper floating down getting caught on the white petals and yellow stamen—blew her smoke in my face and smiled as large as ever she had.

"In that case," she said and cleared her throat, "I guess I'll use my fists."

EMPTY HANDED YEAR

The first time I fingered a girl, I messed it up. Of course, I didn't realize it then. It happened on a Friday night, at a playground. There were four of us there. Two girls, two boys. It was a very open thing. The girl who I fingered said she'd let me try, and we sent our friends to the basketball court to wait for us. They knew what we were up to. It was one of those suburban nights where the clouds seem near yellow against the navy sky. I wore a jacket, Fighting Irish or Los Angeles Kings. She held my shoulders as I explored her. We didn't kiss. Beyond that's mostly a trembly blur.

On Monday morning, I went to school with a short-lived confidence. I entered the cafeteria in search of my friends, and Susan Kang ran to me. "You and Jackie Funk," she said, "up the butt." She held out a finger, made an icky face. My gut swam with confusion.

Back then, I didn't know much. Reflecting, I probably felt vaginas were located in some anatomically impossible space. You ever seen the old TV show *Dallas*? They'd show you the South Fork Ranch house from the outside, and it'd be a mansion, but then they'd show inside, and it'd be an endless castle of a thing. I guess I figured the vagina dwelled in one of those mythical, incapable, interior wings. But Jackie Funk, why didn't you stop me?

Jackie Funk had amazingly hairy arms. She's not dead that I know of, but if she were, this is how she'd be remembered. People wouldn't say it, of course, but they might use a euphemism. "Jackie Funk," they'd say, "sweet as a peach," and there'd be these quiet, guilty smiles that people have when they tease the dead.

Supposedly she'd been caught at a slumber party masturbating with a marker. How could we not be friends? Jackie Funk and me, tight as a pair of crossed fingers. But the accident brought distance to us.

Before that, I'd ride the Dart Bus to her apartment and watch rap videos with her when her mom was away. After, I'm not sure we even spoke on the phone. All she had to do was say, "Stop, you've gone too far," but looking back, I should've known. Something felt strange yet familiar about it. Uninviting. Incorrect.

I'm not upset our relationship tapered, but I am mad Susan Kang advertised my accident to all. For an entire year, I was afraid to hold anything. People would scream taunts at me. I'd have a pen in my hand: "Don't put it up my butt!" I'd have a book in my hand: "Don't put it up my butt!" At lunch I'd be poised to eat a sandwich. "It goes in your mouth," somebody would tell me, "not up my ass." My grades dropped. I lost weight.

Revenge is a bizarre thing because sometimes it just falls in your lap. By odd events I've forgotten, I spent the night at Susan Kang's house a few months later. It was Susan, two other girls and me. The three girls slept in the bed. I slept on the floor closest to Susan. At some point, unprovoked, Susan reached down, put her hands in my pants. There is a strange electricity carried in the first person's hand that touches your penis, and shock shoots through your body in a magical surge. You can hear everything. Your heart. Others' breathing. The movements of the new, foreign hand.

But the hand barely moved. It draped over my member the way a dropped sweater lingers—a complete lack of motion. It stayed still as though dead. For a while, I thought she'd fallen asleep. "Susan," I said, but she answered, "Yes?"

After that, nobody spoke. I lay there with her hand upon me, and felt the electricity drain from the moment, much slower than it came. I wasn't certain what I thought Susan should've done, but I was positive she'd bungled the task, and I'd hoped to broadcast to my friends so Susan would suffer my same fate. I needed retaliation to transpire. I hoped that randomly my friends would lay limp hands on her, inciting embarrassment. But no, it never came.

Before Monday, Susan got it right. With a friend of mine named James who I once was arrested with when we got caught skipping school. He told everyone about Susan and her magical hand while making the gesture Susan didn't provide me, and the two started dating, and I still couldn't hold anything, and at lunch I couldn't eat.

Jackie Funk had large eyes. Brown. Pondering. So large

they seemed lost on her face as we stood beneath those yellow clouds, probably the last time I ever looked directly into them. I don't know why we didn't kiss. I bet she would've let me, but the only thing I can tell you for certain is, the eighth grade was a fucked-up year.

THE LEMONADE TYCOON

I told Robbie Ackerman I was the lemonade tycoon. I said it while I was pissing on his face. I cornered him on the summertime street after chasing him from the sidewalk where his stand rivaled my own. I remember him running from me with a pitcher in each hand, liquid spilling from them. The pitchers fell. Then he fell. And I stood confident above him.

I told him if he didn't let me piss on his face I would kill him. Then he held still as I unzipped my pants.

"I'm the lemonade tycoon," I said, as urine fell steadily.

Then I asked him. I asked him what I was. But he just shook his head and held shut his eyes. I couldn't really blame him. He knew if he answered he'd get piss in his mouth. He'd go to say the words and get a warm mouthful of my sweet, briny waste-water. But I made him say it anyway. Told him if he didn't I'd kick his fucking face in. So he said it. He opened his mouth and the words game gargling out against the stream.

"You're the lemonade tycoon."

Then he started crying and threw up on the pavement and curled like a fetus. I kicked his fucking face in anyway. His nose busted open and his blood puddled alongside the piss and vomit, and he hid his face behind his hands as I smeared him into the puke.

That's why he pushed me out of my wheelchair just now. That's the main reason. There are others.

I used to call Robbie in while I made out with his sister. The Ackermans lived a few houses down from us. His sister was a bit older. Robbie and I were the same age. She wasn't all that pretty. She had a kind of hook nose and wore thick bi-focal glasses. But she had big-warm tits that she'd let me suck on.

I'd go over in the summertime while their parents were at work. She'd invite me into her room, and we'd sit on her bed. She had pink sheets, with white stripes, and she had a stuffed animal collection that she had nestled alongside her pillows.

We'd get to kissing and I'd take off her shirt. I still remember her sour breath, and the softness of her breasts. After a while I'd get bored. She'd never let me go all the way. She'd get short of breath and her pale skin would become splotchy. I'd keep trying for more of her, but she'd always say, "No, no, no." To break up the monotony of denied physical pursuit I'd call little Robbie into the room with the pink sheets, and he'd usually say something like 'Jesus' and try to leave.

I wouldn't have it. I'd make him come back.

"Don't make me chase you down," I'd tell him.

Then he'd reenter and kind of stand in the corner. She'd bury her face into mine and giggle as Robbie's blood boiled and he edged toward the threshold.

He'd slam the door and run once he'd finally built up the nerve to leave, and she'd lay her head back and kind of hum, with her big tits staring up at the ceiling like giant eyeballs loose from their sockets.

When I finally got bored with that I'd steal books from Mr. Ackerman. He had an entire closet filled with Sci-Fi. He had *Star Trek* novels, and *Star Wars* novels, and the whole *Dune* series. My favorites were the *Xanth* series, because Xanth looked like Florida, and that's where my grandma lived.

Robbie Ackerman and I didn't have the same classes in high school. He was an honors student. I was remedial. I'd always see him though. He'd come wandering by while I was roaming the new-addition hallways looking at the pretty girls. His books would be tucked tight beneath one arm. His face looked newly confident.

He snickered at me once as he passed.

"You must be lost," he said. "You couldn't have a class in this hall."

Then one of the pretty girls giggled and suddenly my shirt felt dirty and my back felt hot.

A friend of mine, who had come along to look at all the clean faces, asked me if I was going to take the lip. I, of course, was not. I drove a fist into Ackerman's left ear, and he bounced off a locker and dropped his books on the floor. Then I winked at the girl that had laughed at me, and her mouth fell slightly open, and my friend and I ran in zigzags down the hall.

I dropped out of school shortly after my father lost his job. I was 17. I was a senior. But I knew I wasn't going to go to college anyhow. The whole thing was a waste of my time.

A guy I knew from school worked for a roofer. He got me a gig hauling shingles up ladders. I guess you could say I was an apprentice.

We mostly worked in new subdivisions. The kind where there were only a few lonely houses that stood complete. The rest looked like skeletons surrounded by dirt and white-hot cement.

The days were monotonous. Up and down a wooden ladder heaving shrink-wrapped asphalt shingles upon one shoulder. Most mornings I'd lie still in bed and pray for rain. Rain meant we'd cancel the day. I'd get pissed if it rained in the night and we'd come to the sight to find puddles gathered atop the freshly-tilled earth. That rain did me no good.

One day a shingle slipped from beneath my feet as I walked across a roof. I didn't fall immediately. My legs went racing to find a balance, and I dropped everything that I was holding from my hands. My haphazard course brought me toward the roof-edge where I stepped through an aluminum drip shield and fell. I rotated during the decent, so that I saw first the ground and then the sky above me. Surprisingly the motion felt graceful. Then I heard a crunch and my vision went black.

I had landed back to back with a workhorse beneath me. The fall broke a vertebra in the small of my back. It crushed my thoracic nerve. The injury took away the feeling and movement from my waist to my toes.

"You're lucky you didn't die," the doctor told me.

"Yeah real fucking lucky," I said and my mother cried against my legs.

The Ackermans sent flowers to the hospital. Mrs. Ackerman and my mother knew each other from the neighborhood. The flowers came with a card signed by their whole family. Robbie's name was the biggest. It was the only name I could see. It made something inside me go uncontrollably angry. I puked on my chest. Then I cursed at the nurse as she tried to clean me.

My father disappeared while I was in the hospital. No one is sure where to. He left without saying anything to anyone, but we all kind of agreed it was for the best. The only problem with his departure is that it ensured my mother's role as sole provider for the family. It was a role that was taxing before my accident. It was a role that was impossible thereafter.

My mother and grandmother decided that I would go live in Florida. My grandmother lived in an assisted community. I could get help there from the nurses until I learned to handle my condition. There were still lots of things I could do. I knew that because that's what everyone told me.

Strangers helped me into my seat on the airplane. One of them was a stewardess, one was a passenger. The passenger grabbed my legs, and the stewardess grabbed my shirt, and I could hear people boarding the plane asking, 'What the hell is going on' as the congestion choked their motion to a standstill.

I looked out the window the entire flight. I felt like people on the plane were staring at me. I watched the coastline roll beneath us as we raced through the sky. Everything beneath us looked small.

My grandmother brought several men with her to pick me up at the airport. I learned that Florida was a second love life for old folks. She called all of the men my uncles. Uncle Bob. Uncle Dick. Uncle Tommy.

All of my uncles had tattoos on their arms. All of them had been in the Navy.

We drove home in a forest-green minivan listening to Benny Goodman's chandelier-clean clarinet. Uncle Bob said they didn't make music like they used to. I nodded in agreement and stared hard out the window as pink and blue houses went gliding effortlessly by.

That night we drank cold beers and my uncles cooked steaks. My grandmother sat in my lap and one of the men pushed us around in my wheelchair. My grandmother pretended we were dancing. There was music coming from somewhere.

"I'm so glad you've come to stay," my grandmother told me while one of the uncles spun us in circles. I remember her smelling like dead flowers. I remember her sipping pink wine. She had a loose-fitting red dress on and her skin sagged and wrinkled. Her makeup was thick. Her glasses were thick. She kissed me on the cheek and it felt heavy.

After dinner Uncle Tommy rolled me out onto the back patio which looked out onto a golf course. There was a man on the fairway who Tommy knew. The two men waved at each other. The sun was setting and the sky was orange and pink.

Tommy lit a cigar and asked if I'd like one. I said no and he said suit yourself. He took long exaggerated drags and puffed smoke rings into the air.

"If you end up being a sponge we'll send your ass right back to Texas," Tommy said. "There are worse things than being cripple."

I remained quiet. He was flexing the forearm that had the tattoo. It was an outline of an anchor. It said something I couldn't read.

"Feeling sorry for yourself," he said and chewed at the tip of his thumb. "That's worse."

I set my hands upon my chair wheels. I forced a loose cornered smile. A smoke ring floated down into the line of my vision. I stared through it as the circumference grew. Uncle Tommy patted my shoulder. He spit a piece of tobacco onto the floor. We stayed focused on the distance until the sun sank out toward California. I wished it were taking me with it.

Uncle Tommy told me the names of the constellations when the stars came out, made sure I knew a few of them. Other than that we were quiet.

I fell in love with my nurse the very first second I set eyes on her. She made me wish I'd broken my neck so she'd have more things to help me with. Her name was Sally. She had blonde hair. She was six or seven years older than me. She was engaged.

"You sure you want to marry this guy?" I'd always ask her when she'd come to check my catheter. "Sure I can't make you change your mind."

She'd laugh. Her body was like a spring, tight and alive. She had a permanently sunburned nose. Her hands were smooth and soft. She wore aquamarine scrubs that slipped occasionally on her hips, and she'd reach for them absentmindedly with the tips of her fingers. I'd watch her as she'd touch her waist line. Her shirt would rise slightly. I could see the smallest glimpse of her stomach.

"Let's keep it professional," she'd always say. Then she'd wink at me, and I'd smile.

Sally had access to a transport van. I begged her to take me to the mall. I told her I wanted some new clothes and to go to a pet store. I wanted to get some scorpions to keep in an aquarium.

It took some convincing for my grandmother to let me get them, but she said as soon as I got a job I could get a pet. And I had gotten a job. I sold newspaper subscriptions over the phone. I was perfectly suited for it. I was even good at it.

Sally took me to the mall on her day off. She went around with me while I did my shopping. When you're in a wheelchair you get extra attention from the saleswomen.

They'd all come over to me and ask me if I needed help, and I'd smile at them real big, and get them to suggest things.

"What would look good on me?" I'd ask.

Sally teased me, called me a flirt.

"You're a smooth one," she said.

I just smiled.

"It's easy," I said.

"Why's that?"

"It's fright free. Nothing can happen. I'm like a child scaring a lion from the opposite side of the cage."

She changed the subject. She asked about scorpions.

"They make good pets," I told her.

We went to go find some.

The man at the pet store asked if I knew what I was getting into. He had on a red shirt and a blue vest. He called me young man. I think he thought I was a child.

"They're poisonous, young man" he said. "They can sting you."

"I know," I said. "I'll be super careful." I winked at him and he patted his balding head before ringing up the sale.

I bought two emperor scorpions, an aquarium and crickets to feed them.

On the way home Sally asked if I had sex before the accident. I told her I hadn't. But I told her I'd gotten close. It was quiet for the rest of the drive.

I set up my aquarium as soon as I got to the house. That night I couldn't sleep. I sat awake in my chair until the sun began to show through my window blinds. I teased my new pets from the opposite side of the glass. I did it to pass the time.

It's hard to sell newspapers when you're tired. It's hard to be convincing. I had only slept a few hours. I was nodding off in between calls.

Halfway through the shift my circulation coordinator took a look at my sales sheet.

"What's going on with your numbers?" he asked me. He had a fat neck and wore some cheap department store cologne that I could taste on the edges of my tongue. He had several pens in the front pocket of his white short-sleeve button-up. "Are you using the script?" he asked. "You should stick to the script."

The script was 32 words long.

"Hello, I'm calling from *The Daily Dispatch*. (Ma'am or Sir), you need our paper. Our paper needs you. And with the deals we're offering this month, there's no reason we can't help each other out."

"Yeah I'm using the script," I told him.

"Are you staying positive?" he asked. "You have to stay positive."

I took a deep breath. I thought about my legs.

"I'm a little groggy today," I told him. "Can't seem to get into it."

"Well why don't you go get yourself a coffee, then come back here ready to kick some ass," he said and rubbed my shoulder.

I wheeled myself into the break room and had a cup of black, watery Folgers. It tasted acrid, made my throat itch.

I rolled down to Human Resources before going back to my desk. I had a package that I wanted to send back to Texas.

When I handed it to Rose to put in the outgoing mail she took a look at it. It was a purple box the size of an Acme brick.

"There's no return address," she said.

"I thought it'd make the package look funny," I told her. "It'll either get there or it won't. We'll see if it's meant to be."

She thinned her eyes.

"It's a gift for someone back home," I told her.

I went back to work. The computer called strangers. I tried to sell them papers. Lots of times they'd hang up before I even said hello.

Emperor Scorpions aren't deadly. I know because they didn't kill Robbie Ackerman. And they both stung the shit out of him. At least, that's what my mother told me on the phone.

"Remember little Robbie Ackerman from down the street," she asked me.

"Sure."

"Some asshole sent him scorpions in the mail and he got his fingers stung by both of them."

That was the extent of our conversation. Telephones are weird to me now. I run out of things to say. It'd be a lot easier if I had a script like at work.

Sally gave me an invitation to her wedding one day when she came over to check on me. I told her we should celebrate. She watched me drink a beer on the patio. She couldn't have one. She was on the clock.

The invitation was printed on cream-colored paper. The paper was thick. The words were light purple. I read them to myself. The groom's name was Andre Hector. I hated him.

"Are you sure this is the right guy for you?" I asked.

"One hundred percent certain," she said and placed her hand on my shoulder. That was the last time I ever saw her.

My grandmother died the night before Sally's wedding. She died in her sleep. I tried to call Sally to tell her. She didn't answer. I suppose she was busy.

She didn't come to my grandmother's funeral. She was on her honeymoon. But my mother flew in, and my uncles all came, and there were people from the assisted community that showed up to give sympathies. Mostly the old people just talked about who had died recently. It must suck to become old.

The minister was old. The organist was old. An old woman sang a sad song. Her vibrato calisthenics twitched and faltered during the bridge. She was dressed in a red robe. So was the minister. He went on for an hour. I have no idea what he said.

After the funeral Uncle Tommy came up to me and knelt down so that we were eye to eye.

"Well," he said. "You weren't a sponge."

Then an old woman came up and shook my hand. I could feel the bones of her fingers grinding into my flesh. She rubbed her palms so deep into mine that it seemed she was trying for the backs of our hands to meet on the inside. It felt like she wanted to steal my youth.

"Your grandmother and I were best-dear friends," she told me. "I lived just down the road from her."

"That's weird," I told her. "I've been staying with my grandmother for three months, and I've never seen you."

The woman looked confused. She smelled like mothballs. Her skin was grey. One of my uncles came up beside her and told her not to mind me. He told her I was taking it pretty hard. They left together shortly after that.

There was no other choice but for me to go back to Texas. We booked flights. We left the next day.

My mother read magazines on the plane trip home. The magazines were all about celebrities. There were pictures of women whose bones came screaming out through their flesh. One of them had giant glasses that covered half of her face and blonde stringy hair that fell coarsely from an oversized beanie.

My mother thought she was gorgeous. I could tell because she paused for a long time on the page and looked the woman over in detail.

"You've gotten skinny," I told my mom. She said thank you.

My mother's new boyfriend came to pick us up at the airport. His name was Larry. My mom told me he was a sailor. I asked if he had been in the Navy. He hadn't. He didn't have any tattoos.

We seemed to be making all the wrong turns on the way home.

"Where are we going?"

"I've moved in with Larry," Mom said. "I got rid of the house. We'll be staying with him."

Larry looked at me in the rearview mirror. I was in the backseat. My chair was in the trunk.

"You're gonna love it," he told me.

We pulled into the marina. There were boats docked in the water. They rose. They fell.

We pulled up to a two-tiered house boat. It was painted white.

Larry took the key from the ignition. He clicked his tongue and opened his car door.

"What are we doing?"

"We're home," Mom said.

It was awkward getting me onto the boat. There was a ramp, but my chair was too wide for it. I had to be carried aboard. My mother and Larry each grabbed me under the armpit. Then they walked me sideways up the ramp.

My room was a small cabin on the first floor. There was no way for me to get around unless I walked on my hands. Larry and my mother went to pick up dinner from a Chinese restaurant downtown. I stayed behind. I sat on my bed. The boat bobbed up and down as the water licked upon the hull walls. I could hear the water. I could hear seagulls screaming in the air as they looked for floating trash. I felt nauseous.

My mother and Larry returned a few hours later. They had several cartons of Chinese food and Tsingtao beer. They helped me to the kitchen table and we ate our dinner on paper plates, drank the beer out of the bottles.

"You know who's still in town?" my mother asked me.

I had no idea.

"Little Robbie Ackerman," she told me and I shrugged. "He goes to the A&M here. I told his mother you were coming home, and she said the two of you should get together. I know you two were friends, growing up down the street from each other and all."

"Sure."

"Larry and I are going to take you by there tomorrow night," she told me.

"What?"

"By Robbie's," she said and took a sip of her beer. "He's going to take you out on the town. To a party or something."

I had a hard time sleeping that night. I woke up every time the boat moved.

Larry and my mother did not wait for me to enter the Ackerman's. They helped me into my chair and drove away quickly. I rolled myself up the driveway, down a cement path, and up to the front of the house. I didn't have to knock. The lock turned and Robbie Ackerman opened the door. He was quiet. We were both quiet. Then he smiled and told me to come in.

I rolled myself into the entry. I hadn't been inside since my freshman year. I quit coming around to see Robbie's sister once she got a steady boyfriend. I think he was on the chess team.

Once she invited me over while they were dating. I saw her in the halls at school and she told me not to be a stranger. She gave me a look, but I never obliged her.

Robbie said he was the only one home, but I thought I saw light coming from underneath her bedroom door.

Robbie took me to a keg party at one of the university dorms. We were quiet the whole way. He had a small pickup truck. I pulled myself into the cab using the oh-shit handle. Then he put my chair in the bed and slammed the tailgate. The truck shook.

We drove alongside the bay. The moon was full. The reflection shone bright on the water. There was a song on the radio I'd never heard. For the past couple of months I'd been listening to old-people music.

"Who's this?" I asked and pointed to the radio. Robbie didn't answer. He looked out the window at the water.

When we got to the party Robbie put my chair on the cement and then opened my door. I lowered myself into the wheelchair. Robbie didn't wait for me. He walked into the party alone.

I debated leaving, but it would have been a long way back to Larry's boat, and I doubted there would be sidewalks the entire way.

A girl with blonde hair held the door open for me once I finally decided to go in. She gave me an awkward look of sympathy as I wheeled by. I wondered if we had ever met.

I ended up sitting beside a couch in the living room. A big dude wearing a tank top brought me a beer.

"Here you go bro," he said. I drank the beer. I remained quiet.

People kept moving around at the party. They'd go from room to room. The scenery kept changing. The girls were beautiful. Very few of them spoke to me.

One girl, however, did come up.

"Oh my, God," she said. "You got into college." Her mouth dropped open. Then I recognized her. It was the girl that watched me punch Ackerman's ear.

"No," I told her. "I don't go to school."

Then I rolled myself outside. I don't think she realized I was in a wheelchair.

Robbie was out front. He was standing in a huddle of guys smoking. I thought about going up to him and asking for a lift home, but I didn't want to owe him anything, so I just began to roll away.

I crossed a parking lot and turned behind a school building. It was quiet. The air smelled like salt.

I sat there in the shadows with my arms crossed. I leaned my head back. My throat felt tight. My legs didn't feel anything.

I heard a noise from behind me. I grabbed my left wheel and pulled back so I spun 180 degrees.

Robbie Ackerman was standing there. He was short of breath. He must have run to find me.

"What are you doing?" he asked.

"Looking at the stars," I told him. "Do you know much about the constellations?"

"A little," he said.

"I was looking for Scorpius," I said and began to laugh.

I heard movement. Then I felt a fist drive into the top of my head.

"You mother fucker," he screamed. "It was you."

I wheeled myself forward. It felt good that he hit me. I began to laugh. The laughter seemed to come up from my feet like a fuzzy reverse-venom. I wanted him to hit me again.

"Oh, shit," I said. "Oh, shit that stung."

I pivoted so that we were face to face.

"Hey remember that time I punched your ear?" I asked. I pulled my hands up to my chest. It felt like webs of warmth were running through my body, and I was laughing so hard my stomach hurt.

Robbie dove at me and swung his fist twice. The first blow

landed on my cheek. The second one busted my nose open. Blood fell down upon my chest. My chair rolled backward. I felt proud and intense like white-hot light. I could always get him to do whatever I wanted.

I cupped my hands beneath my face. I could feel them filling with blood. I could taste the metallic bite of it in my mouth as I laughed, and the flavor swayed like a palm tree.

It took me a while to catch my breath. Robbie just stood there.

"Remember the time I pissed on your face?" I asked. My sides ached from laughter. He lunged at me and kicked. It looked silly, but the force pushed my chair and I fell from the seat. My hands hit the cement. My skin scraped off against the rough surface. Then my chin hit. It felt warm.

"You're a piece of shit," Robbie said as I rolled on the ground. It sounded funny to hear him cuss. "I'm fucking done with you."

But he wasn't done with me. Because I didn't want him to be.

My vision blurred. My whole body ached. But I wanted something. I needed more. I could see his silhouette. It was moving away.

"Hey, Robbie," I yelled, and began laughing again. I was trying to push myself up on my elbows. "Hey, Robbie!"

He stopped. I could barely breathe.

"What?" he asked.

I was bleeding, but it was hysterical. Everything felt graceful. The pain and the laughter and the blood.

"What?"

"I want you to do me a favor," I said.

He didn't move.

"What's that?" he asked. He sounded winded. I spat on the ground. I was spitting blood.

"Tell me that I'm the Lemonade Tycoon."

Then he turned and came back toward me.

STAMP # 2

At the window, with it open, as rain sang across the land once dry, so the rain slipped in threads of current down cracks and toward the lows, the man wiped his glasses free of spray—beads that had hit the sill and splattered at him. He cleared his throat, put the glasses back on, picked up a cigarette weaving smoke into the pale-yellow room—a light cast by a single bulb dangling above the kitchen table from a cord, makeshift.

"Would you say," said the man now ashing his cigarette, smoke staining his words, his eyes toward the rain, "that I am very brave?" He then looked at the woman, wrapped in a blanket, her eyes tight against the chill, her body frail with age and labor, her hair winced gray by days. She tightened the blanket across her shoulders, leaned against a wall—faded white paint, cracked and spotting.

"These days?" she said, and looked now at the rain, sighed

as if she knew it only came to wash her off the land, to hoist their home from its foundation in a torrent toward the death of it—nature ravaging its boards and bones to splinters and shingles and scraps and refuse that would toss wildly in the breath of flood until it came to rest unrecognizable. She closed her eyes. Turned from the man. "I wouldn't even call you handsome."

Recently the couple bickered, made fights from moments others might let pass silently, but in the past they would hold hands until the warmth of their palms birthed a slickness from sweat, but even then their fingers stayed clasped through the damp. They'd speak cute phrases to each other—the man warmly cooing her name, the woman smiling when she heard him coo it. But that music had faded from them.

The man looked at the woman, nodded, said, "I'm ugly," he said, "but ugly men can live bravely."

"They can," said the woman, and she stayed silent a moment so only the sound of rain filled the room, and she looked at the man, lazily blinked her eyes, smiled so slightly only she could sense it. "But I've never seen it."

The man shrugged. He ashed his cigarette mildly. He turned back toward the rain. They didn't speak for a long time.

TAKE ME WITH YOU

My brother had a strange way of touching me, and when I tell that to people they nod knowingly as though this reveals some secret motive for his despicable actions, but it wasn't spooky like they think. If you're puzzled, thank goodness. Where you from? Take me with you? Everyone in the Coastal Bend knows Stuart Kipper, knows how he walked into the Suffering Brotherhood chapel and opened fire on the unfortunate worshipers there. It was on the news, even nationally. They had a video of him carrying two shotguns and a duffel bag slung over his shoulder—his newly-shaved head shining where it wasn't scabbed up by his haphazard razor job.

This was a dozen years back, but I'm sure the hurt of all that sits fresh on those people's families' minds, just as I still pine for my brother, especially at Christmas. The hurt of an untimely death will last as long as it wants to, and even though my brother was the architect of his demise—putting himself in a situation that led to his being shot—I wish he was here. In some ways, even if he had to do what he did, I wish maybe he'd just been apprehended, so I could've spoken to him one last time before they gave him lethal injection up at Walls—he and I chatting on those black one-way phones as we sat on the opposite sides of bullet-proof glass, swallowing the thickness of it.

Know what I would've asked him: What the fuck, man?

These days, I've quit getting death threats, and, honestly, those only ever came by phone and never really worried me much. I had a shrink for a bit and he wondered if I shouldn't move away from Corpus Christi. "Go get a fresh start." But how? It's not like I can sell the store for any amount that'd sustain me.

Here's a quick geography lesson: part of my town's a piece of shit, and the part that is is where my father started a corner store called Kipper's. Sure we're down by the bay close enough to taste the salt off the water, but you can also smell the fumes from the refineries, so no one wants to be here but the seagulls who caw madly and waddle round my dumpster pecking garbage. My brother and I ran Kipper's up until his death. I run it alone now. My sister wants no part. She's married, got a new last name that's served her well, pretends she's never been a Kipper. I don't blame her. I've thought about changing the name myself, but it seems like a hassle. I'd have to go down to the courthouse and explain why to the judge. I've also thought about changing the store name upon a time, but new signage would cost a chunk, and it seems like enough years have elapsed that the bad memory of the Suffering

Brotherhood might be behind me. And, yes, I understand how that sounds. Some churches are just named perfectly. By the by, it's gone now. Closed up. Torn down. Nothing there but an asphalt lot. Hand-painted sign giving a phone number to call if you're interested in purchasing. I called a bit back just to see what they're asking for it, cause I'm always amazed how prices around here have plummeted. Got a fax machine that chirped computer language at me. Round Christmas, people lay flowers where the chapel used to be. Across town, in the good neighborhoods, folks have already put their lights out. Earlier each year, it seems. Holiday season's just a sour note to me.

So, maybe you're like: your brother's touch?

Sure, sure. You deserve an explanation.

It starts with David Sparks who grew up on the same street we did and who was deaf. I only remember seeing him twice. Once when he played football with us when we first moved into the house, and once when he got hit by a Trans Am and got his leg broke right before his folks sent him away to a state school. I'm guessing he got hit because he couldn't hear it coming. He was several years older than us, and the kid had an arm. The time we played football, after he left, my brother said, "If he could hear I bet he'd play college QB."

I don't remember well enough to say, but I do remember this: David couldn't speak a word. This he intimated to us somehow, but what was amazing was how he gave us plays. David played full-time QB, that is to say, he played for both teams. There was me, my brother, some of my cousins and some of the neighborhood kids, and I'm not sure how it all got sussed out, but there were two teams of us that David captained, and he didn't hand off shit. We had some kind of silent count five-Mississippi that the defenses had to abide by before rushing him, and all the other members of the team aside from David ran routes. How'd we know the routes to run? That's where the touch comes into play. David would call a huddle, but we'd be facing the other team, and he'd draw the routes he'd want us to run on our backs with his finger. All X's and O's. He'd tap your X twice to let you know it was you, then he'd draw you out the route to run. He'd hike the ball and you'd tear off, trying to get open. That was the only time we ever played with him like that, but it stuck with my brother hard, and he'd often come up behind me and draw routes on my back for no reason. Then we'd laugh. I don't know whatever happened to David. My brother got shot in the face.

After it happened, my sister gave me shit.

"He didn't seem funny to you? Didn't seem odd?"

This is a question I still field, when I'm out and about, running into old school friends at department stores buying sneakers. I can only shrug at it. I've torn my mind open looking for clues I missed, and the only thing that seems to occur to me was something he said the day before.

We were in the back of Kipper's feeding cardboard into the incinerator for one of the final times. It wasn't legal doing it, but at night no one could tell. He had the door of it open and was watching the orange fire, his face aglow so his eyes seemed sunk back into shadows, and he looked at me, said, "Ever think you were born in the wrong century?" At the time, I thought he meant because the incinerator. Because used to be everyone used them but they'd been regulated against. I truly don't remember how I responded. I let my employees take cigarette breaks back there now. They blow their smoke out the flue. Other than that it hasn't been used in twelve years. Of course, it still smells like fire.

For about a year after it happened, every so often, kids at night would vandalize the store. They'd come around with paint cans, brushes, a ladder I guess. They'd haul up to the signage and deface it. Paint it so it said Killer's instead of Kipper's. Kind of witty, really.

My sister saw that once, said, "You have to close. Think about those people's families."

I did. All the time. My brother killed eight people. One of them was a baby. He shot the thing as it slept in a stroller at nearly point-blank. My sister's own kid was a baby at the time, now a freshman at Richard King, plays point guard JV. The weekend before my brother did it, he gave my nephew a bath in my mother's kitchen sink. Sang "Rubber Ducky" to the little guy as he washed behind his ears.

In 1966 Charles Whitman killed his wife and mother and climbed to the top of the clock tower at UT-Austin and shot down at anyone he could target. In total, he killed 16, injured over 30. In a suicide note, he requested an autopsy because he couldn't understand his motivation for these acts of heinousness, and he hoped science might reveal why he was so compelled. Turns out, he had a tumor the size of a pecan in his brain. After my brother's death, and before his cremation, similar studies were made of my brother's corpse. Doctors explored his insides, they tested his piss and blood. I kept hoping they'd find something, even played out conversations in my mind. "Like the guy in Austin?" someone might say when I told of the discovery. "Just the same." If only they'd found a tumor, then we could've all just blamed God.

Here are the bestselling items at Kipper's, year in and year out: Beer, Cigarettes, Milk, Bread. Everything else we have is for convenience. I'm serious. I probably lose money just putting other things out. I could downsize, hunker my stock into a corner of Kipper's and sell nothing but Beer, Cigarettes, Milk and Bread and make more money than ever. All the tired mothers and stumbling drunks would still come just the same, but can you imagine looking out at all that repulsive honesty: The pared-down sincerity of the basest wants and needs? Besides, every so often, I'll be in the aisles stocking the shelves and some wayward customer will come up curious about whether or not we've got batteries or Spam, and they'll touch my back with a finger, like to get my attention, and even though all these years have gone, I still think for a split second that maybe it's my brother, come up behind to draw a route on my back.

The college kids have started coming around with their fake ID's, so school must be out for winter. They come down to Kipper's because it's a shit hole, and they think, rightfully so, that we have lower standards when checking driver's licenses. When I was younger, I had my brother's expired one, and in some ways I think it's sort of my duty to let that tradition live on. Was a time, I'd even pretend to be him. I'd be at the counter with beer and the cashier'd be suspicious. "What's your name?" they'd ask me. "Stuart," I'd tell them. Today, a boy came in to buy a twelve of Lite. "Home from school?" I asked. He nodded. "Which one?" He told me UT-Austin. You see, everyone can be linked to a murderer somehow.

Now, even the neighbors have their lights out, strings of white bulbs fragile as far-away stars. I see them when I take out trash, twinkling from their distance. You know, it costs me money to recycle. I pay the city to take my old boxes down to a center where I guess they turn it to pulp for other products. More and more I see our inventory is made from re-used paper. Burning was always free. You'd take all the paper back to the incinerator, get bits going like kindling, feed stuff in slow to not choke out the blaze, keep piling it on and watch it float off as smoke. But, of course, nothing's ever gone forever. I guess the ash would come down elsewhere, stain the beaches and rivers, tarnish lungs, cause our cancers. My brother's ashes are spread in Corpus Christi Bay. No one seemed to care much about that.

The Christmas after my brother did that killing, the pastor from the Suffering Brotherhood came into the store in his little church outfit. He was a stubby, bald man who looked like he had secrets. I was a bit drunk on malt liquor, because this was back when I was drinking, and he stood at my register with his hands folded and said, "I forgive you." I told him I didn't do a fucking thing to be forgiven for, and he nodded in some knowing manner, said, "I forgive you," again. I think I threw something at him, but I really can't remember.

There are flowers in the parking lot where the chapel once sat, so I'm guessing it's the day of: I ignore calendars this time of year. I stopped on my way to work to contemplate them—red roses limped in a pile between two sun-drained yellow lines that once marked a parking space. Seemed a tacky color for them to be, but they hummed colorfully beneath the mottled-gray sky. Seagulls staggered around them, looking for food. As I stood there, I felt a touch on my back, turned to look and some stranger apologized to me. "You family too?" they asked. I nodded, and they hugged me. "You know," they said, "I'm just happy they killed the monster who did it. All these years," they said, "and that's the only thing that gets me by."

"Yeah," I told them. "Makes it a bit easier for everyone, I suppose."

When I got into Kipper's there was a message for me to return a phone call, and I assumed someone else had realized the anniversary and wanted to tell me to go to hell, but I was wrong.

I dialed the number and it was some realtor said they'd seen my number on caller ID.

"Oh, yeah. I'd called about the lot on Chisolm."

"The old church?"

"I don't know," I lied.

"For the price," he said. "It's a great property. For the price," he said, "it really can't be beat."

"Tell me everything you know about it," I said. I sat down, got comfortable. "And not just a little bit, you hear. Tell me every, single thing."

"Well," he said, and he told me the lot size, and he told me the zoning, and he gave me the price. "Other than that," he said, "there's not much to tell. Unless you have some specific question?"

"Just one," I said, "but it's kind of a doozy."

"Shoot."

"Ever think you were born in the wrong century?"

The phone went silent. Static hummed between us.

"Is that a riddle?" he said. "I don't think I understand."

I nodded at him, even though he couldn't see it. "That's okay," I told him. "Neither did I." I thanked him for his time.

I told him I wasn't interested.

"No problem," he said. "Sometimes you just gotta hear a thing to know whether or not it's meant for you." He told me to remember him, just in case I changed my mind. Of course, I'm pretty certain that's a thing I'll never do.

WAXING

When I was twenty-one my best friend broke his neck. It was
at his nineteenth birthday party, and I didn't buy the liquor for
it. Some rich kid's dad had just been released from Canadian
prison for pushing his father down the stairs, killing him, so
we were told. I guess after all that time locked away, the idea
of a party sounded fine to him, so he stocked his garage fridge
with Coors Light, and we went over to swim in their pool.
My friend drove over before me. I caught a ride with a girl my
best friend was crushing on, but he had known her too long
or she had seen him in the wrong light, and when she pointed
to the moon, a sliver of white crescent, and said, "Cheshire
Cat smile," and looked at me through thinning eyes, a smirk
on her face, I knew I could kiss her, and I did.

It worked like this: we were out front kissing, alone.
Everyone else was in their bathing suits or by the pool drunk

and laughing. It's hard to be certain, but I remember the night cold, so everyone in the water must have been buzzed enough not to care. My friend didn't care at all.

It was an awkward little pool. We didn't know at the time. It was four feet deep all the way across. A lap pool. A wasted, waist-high pool.

All the stories are jumbled, but what I think I've decided, is that my friend got out of what he thought was the shallow end, dived head-first into what he thought was the deep end. But it didn't exist. His head hit the bottom. His neck snapped on contact, I hope.

The only other way it could've happened is this: when I came into the backyard there was no idea my friend's neck had been hurt. "He was drowning," this kid said, "I pulled him out." I did CPR on him. I balled my right fist, set it against the back of my left hand, and set my left palm to his chest. I compressed. Five times, and then I blew breath in his mouth, his lips sloppy wet with chlorine water. I did this a while, and then some kid, shaved head and an adrenalin look about him, relieved me of compressions, and I only did the breathing. "Let's lift him up," someone said, and we did, but his body was slick. He floundered away from us, and his head smacked dead against the concrete pool-side surface. We lifted him again, his head bobbing to and fro. Water drained from his mouth in a thick stream.

"I think he's okay," someone said.

The rich kid's father, who had come out of the house when he heard the commotion, added, "I heard him say he was fine."

"I didn't hear anything," I said.

"I think," said the rich kid's father, "we should put him in the bed in the pool house," he motioned to a sort of finished club house near us, "let him sleep it off."

At this point I was on wet knees looking up at him—the moon in the sky above, several stars whose names I didn't know, the sweet chemical smell of the pool. "I'm driving him to the hospital," I said.

A friend of mine, which one it's hard to say, asked, "You think he needs it?"

Then I said the stupidest thing I've ever said. "Does it look like I know medicine?" Thinking back on it, I'm not even certain what that sentence means, but it clings to me.

Then I heard the most magical thing I've ever heard: "We need an ambulance." They were radiant, those words. Some bright girl had used a cell phone to call 911. It made so much sense it crippled me.

This was 1999. People didn't just have cell phones. These days, sure. Everyone walks around with a computer in their pocket. A portal to all answers, but then, no. Barely anyone. It didn't take long for help to arrive. The paramedics ushered us out of the backyard. We stood in the front beside the ambulance, the lights spinning, throwing reds and blues all across the night.

The rich kid was leaned against a car grinning. "Something funny?" I asked him.

He looked down at the ground, ashamed. "No," he said. "I don't know what's wrong with me."

The air smelled of pine. I held the hand of the girl my friend liked. "It's taking forever," she said.

"That's a good sign," one of her girlfriends told her, which I now know to be a lie. She was chewing gum, blew a bubble, let it pop, chewed again. "If he were really messed up, they'd throw him in the back of that ambulance and get him to the hospital fast as they could."

They had to stabilize his neck before they could move him, drain his lungs of water. But then, we were under the impression that he'd only quit breathing, not that he was broken.

Once he was loaded, and they drove him away, my friend's crush took me home. We called the hospital, but they wouldn't give us information.

The girl didn't let me kiss her anymore, but I tried to once or twice. I wanted her to stay over, but she left me at my apartment to sit on my fake-leather sofa alone.

The next day I went to another friend's apartment on Fourth Street. His mother was in town, and I had her call the hospital. She shook her head when she got off the phone, "All I can tell you," she said, "is if he lives, he won't be the same."

I had to work that afternoon at Amy's Ice Cream, and I only remember that because I had my manager drive me by my best friend's apartment after my shift so I could clean it out. He had a bong and some hash and a few liquor bottles that I was sure he wouldn't want his parents to see, and I got rid of everything that would embarrass him, tossed his nudey magazines, erased his Internet history.

The girl he liked called that evening. She had talked to my best friend's mother. "He's going to live," she said, and my eyes went wet when she said it.

We talked a while, and, when we got off the phone, she

told me she loved me, but when I said it back she was gone.

I didn't have a car then, because my license was suspended. Every day for two weeks I'd take the number seven bus south down Duval and get off at MLK. From there I'd walk to the hospital and sit in my best friend's room, watch the machines breathe for him. His father came up from Corpus Christi. He kept having me tell him the story. I left out the part about kissing the girl.

My best friend and I were enrolled in classes at the community college, and I got the papers his father needed to sign so he'd be dropped. "You won't forget him, will you?" his father asked me and motioned to my friend who slipped in and out of consciousness and could only answer yes or no with his eyes. We didn't know how much he'd recover. We knew he'd never walk.

"Of course not," I said. "How could I?"

At the end of two weeks they moved him to a hospital in a city it took four hours to drive to.

I kept calling the girl. She kept not answering, not returning my calls.

That winter I moved to Winooski, Vermont. I only stayed two months. Lake Champlain froze over and people drove onto the ice to drill holes and fish. I asked a man at a bar on Church Street what happened when cars went through.

"They don't often," he said, "but when they do, they give you twenty-four hours to get 'em out of the lake."

"What happens if you can't?" I asked.

"They take away your license for a year," he said.

"You ever seen someone lose their car and fish it out?" I asked. "No," he said. "But I keep hoping."

I was supposed to go to culinary school there, but I couldn't stand the winter. The snow and the cold was fine, but the sun didn't rise until nearly 9:00 AM and it set around 4:00 in the evening, and I moped around too much thinking about my friend and the girl who wouldn't call me, and I drove home to Texas in a blizzard listening to Elliott Smith.

The last time I saw my old best friend he was living in an apartment the color of roach wings, and his refrigerator had pools of standing water on the shelves. He smoked weed and we watched a movie, and he had all these pills he had to take, and the guy who took care of him did curls with weights that made him grunt and groan.

He asked about the girl I'd kissed. He didn't know I'd kissed her, and I didn't tell him. I didn't know anything about her, and he knew the same.

There were others he asked about too. What were they doing? Where had they moved?

I didn't know most of the people he asked about. I probably had once, but I forget a lot of things.

Ten years after my friend broke his neck, I saw the girl I kissed on a rooftop bar in downtown Austin, Texas, and she wore a tight black tank top, and somehow she recognized me. She came over, asked about "the kid who broke his neck."

"He's back home," I told her. "Living in a retirement home," I said. "I need to go see him."

"It's terrible what happened," she said. "To him." I nodded.

"Want a drink?" I asked. "I'm going up to the bar."

Some formless music swirled around us, the space lit as if with Christmas lights.

"No," she said. "I'm fixing to head out with some friends." She smiled at me. "It was an accident," she said.

"I know," I told her, "but I still feel bad about it."

"It's just," she said, "back then I was talking to my mom a lot."

I was confused, and she could see it in my face.

"On the phone," she said. "And," she said, "whenever I'd get off the phone with her I'd tell her I loved her," she frowned. "That's why I said it."

"How do you remember that?" I asked. She shrugged her shoulders, walked away and talked with friends.

It was really a waxing crescent, the moon. Not a smile. Tonight it's the same and it's winter. Most likely Lake Champlain is frozen over. Cars perched on the ice, and I hope one slips through. If I had a car break the ice, I'd not go after it. It would slush to the bottom of the frozen lake, and before it even hit the bottom, I'd forget its color, and they could take my license for a year. Besides, if you got it out, you know it'd never work the same.

I don't have a best friend now, but I'm married.

When the moon's like this, I think it all back. I stand alone in the yard, my eyes at the sky.

It's funny. Right now, my hands are in my pockets. What if I could never use them?

I stand still in the night trying to forget the feel of my body, until my wife calls me to come inside.

I wish I could say this is unusual.

I can't tell you how many times it's happened.

A RANDOM MIGRATION

Tommy Bishop had died, and I didn't care. I hadn't seen him in years, and I'd only missed him once. It was on a visit back home. I'd gone out to a dive bar—black walls, fluorescent lighting, an off-balance pool table. I got whiskey bent with some girls from high school who asked about Bishop because they knew we'd been friends. I talked about him a bit—told about the time he set the principal's car on fire. We laughed and raised a glass to him.

The last thing I heard, before I heard he died, was he'd been popped running weed in some place north like Montana. When he died, people I couldn't remember called me on the phone.

"Hear about Bishop?" they'd ask, and I'd say what I knew.

First story I got was from Larry the wine guy. I'd known him back home when we were kids. He'd come into the kitchen looking for my chef. I didn't like him much. He was awkward. His head hung too far in front of his body. His step was too side to side. He looked like he was searching for a lost dog or late taking medication.

"Heard Bishop hanged himself?" he said and pulled an imaginary rope above him. Then, "Chef around?"

I motioned toward the office.

Larry bobbed his head, rubbed his hands together, gaited off like an ice skater—up and down, side to side.

My mother told me later that Bishop burned to death in a fire.

I called her on the sly from the walk-in during service and my phone had a bad connection. I heard everything twice, through some digital echo.

"Did you read it in the paper?" I asked. *The paper, the paper.*

"No," she told me. "From a woman at church." *At church, at church.*

So I made another call to a friend I'd once cooked with and he said it was murder.

"Pissed somebody off," he told me. "The wrong somebody."

"Where'd it happen?"

"Port Aransas."

"When he get back to Texas?"

"Beats me."

"Who'd burn someone to death?"

"Hell if I know."

That was it. That was all I knew. But for whatever reason, I kept thinking up memories.

September 1996. The newspaper called them butterflies, but I didn't see it. They looked like locusts crossing over the bay. Their black wings seemed to beat in unison. There were millions. They clouded the horizon, blotted out the blue sky, looked like rain sweeping in from the north.

We knew they were coming because we'd heard it from news casts, and through phone calls from cities out toward San Antonio, and we'd seen pictures of car grills pasted with thick mounds of lifeless wings on the Internet at school.

My teacher told us they were thirsty, explained it was because of drought.

Bishop came and grabbed me in the hall, said we had to go see them.

Back then neither of us had a car. We recruited this girl Gia to cut school with us because she had a ride. She didn't want to come at first.

"My dad finds out he'll take away my car."

But Bishop laid his hand on her shoulder. "You're daddy won't ever know nothing." He smiled and her eyes fell slightly and I knew she was in.

One of the security guards at my high school moonlighted as a butcher at the grocery store where I worked. Nobody liked her, but I'd seen her different at the other job. Sometimes we'd sneak beers together or smoke cigarettes while burning boxes, blowing our cigarette smoke up through the incinerator flue.

Sometimes she'd stare at me and tell me how lucky I was. Once she touched my lips with her finger and started to laugh. I just stood there silently sipping at my beer and feeling warm from the fire.

Usually, she'd let me leave campus without too much hassle, so we didn't worry when she came up to the car.

"Where you think you're going?" she asked when we pulled up to the exit.

"Going to go watch the butterflies come in," I told her.

I was sitting in the back seat on the driver's side with the window down. She reached in, patted my cheek.

"You're such a child," she said. She shook her head and stared at Gia. Then she waved us on. "Be careful," she told us.

"Always are," Bishop hollered. He turned on the radio as the car pulled from the parking lot.

We drove down to the waterfront and parked near the sea wall. The bay was glass, the sky vacantly blue, we were the only ones there. But none of that matters, or it sits far away from what happened next.

I'd like to say it was dramatic, but I can't. It was a slow thing. The air was still, somehow, no breeze, and the bugs looked like filth flying in an up and down way, like bits of char coming off a bonfire, catching current, rising and falling.

When they neared, Gia screamed, "I'm getting back in the car." But Bishop caught her wrist, wouldn't let her.

I shut my eyes for a moment as the butterflies surrounded us, and I felt wings against my arms and chest. When I opened my eyes I was engulfed in a sea of slow black bugs.

Bishop grabbed on, held it for us to see. It had a long snout, and a quick stroke of brown up the front of its wing. When he let it go, it couldn't fly. It fell to the ground, and ran in circles until Bishop stepped on it.

Gia punched his shoulder, but he just smiled, and I wandered down to the cement steps, sat there as salt water sprayed my shoes, counting the oil derricks in the bay and watching the gulls dive at the butterflies.

After a few minutes Bishop called me.

"Bo," he screamed. "We're out."

We got back into Gia's car and drove downtown to a liquor store where Bishop knew a guy we could buy from, but he had to go in alone.

I stayed in the car with Gia. I could see her face in the rear-view mirror. She had large, hazel eyes and skin the color of light-brown sugar. We had held hands the summer before while sitting on a bean bag chair, but Bishop had claimed her so I was too afraid to do anything else.

She saw me looking at her and winked. I sort of smiled.

"So," she said, "what's up with you and the security guard?"

"She works at the grocery with me."

"That's all?"

"Fuck you," I said, and she laughed and laughed.

Bishop bought three bottles of fruit-flavored wine and a small flask of bourbon. By now the butterflies were downtown, people walked around taking pictures.

We drove to the U.S. Service Building parking lot. We were underage drinking and hiding in plain sight. The garage had steep, angled inclines from one floor to the next, and on the final ascent we faced straight into a sky sprinkled with butterflies.

We passed the bourbon around, chased the hot liquor with the sweet flavored wine.

When I tried to hand the bottle back to Bishop he squeezed my hand and motioned with his head. I nodded, pocketed the flask and opened the car door.

"I'm gonna go spit on the street," I said, because I couldn't think of anything else to say.

I got out of the car and walked to the edge of the building. I looked out across downtown. The streets were choked with butterflies and people who had come out to see them. I took a sip of bourbon. It was warm and heavy. I swallowed several times after it had gone down. I didn't like the taste, but I liked the warm rush that climbed up from my belly and across my limbs. I took a deep breath. I could taste the salty air of the bay in the back of my throat. There were seagulls diving at the butterflies and screeching. Car horns floated up from the road.

When I turned around Gia's car was rocking. I folded my arms and leaned into the parking garage wall.

Chef called me into his office after the dinner rush. It was a small room with a computer on a card table and stacks of recipe books in the corners. He poured himself a snifter of Cognac and motioned for me to sit. He crossed his legs and leaned into his own chair and shook his head while looking at me.

"What the fuck?" he asked.

Chef was from Holland and his accent made him sound like a deaf person who learned to talk by holding his hand against somebody's throat. He hated everything except cigarettes, cooking and liquor. Sometimes he'd sit on a bench behind the restaurant blowing smoke and staring out into space.

His wife had fake tits and she would always get drunk with

the customers and take them out dancing. I figured that's what he thought about as he sat by himself. He was gaining weight. He was losing hair. He was drunk every day.

"You on phone in cooler talking. Absent minded. Head up ass," he said.

"Sorry," I told him. "Found out an old friend died."

"Ah," he said, and took a sip of his Cognac. "Life is shit, no?"

I smiled and nodded.

"Listen," he said. "I must ask question. I need truth."

"Of course Chef," I said. "You can ask me anything."

"Will you be okay without job?"

"Everything okay?"

"I'm closing," he told me.

"What," I was relieved. I thought he was going to ask me about his wife.

"Yes," he said and touched the wall with his finger. "This place, I hate it."

"When?"

"Immediately. No more restaurant. No more Chef."

"What will you do?" I asked him.

"Go back to Holland, maybe. I've not decided."

We shook hands, and I told him I'd get my things and leave. I heard his wife later. She was crying in the office as I cleaned and put away my knives. I called my mom and said I was gonna take a trip to come see her in the morning.

I didn't see Gia for a while after the day with the butterflies. Somehow her dad found out and took away her car. She was pissed at Bishop. She was pissed at me.

Then one night she called me on the phone. She asked me to come over. I only lived a few blocks away, so I made the walk.

It was fall. The air felt fresh. It had been raining. The asphalt streets were slick and puddled and the surface glistened with street-lamp light.

Gia didn't want me to come to the door. I knocked on her window and waited until she could climb out. I said, "What's up?" when she finally slipped from the window ledge. She put her fingers to her lips, took my hand, led me out of her yard.

She led me to a small park that was tucked into a row of houses. We walked toward the playground and both sat down on swings.

She stared at me.

"What?" I asked.

She leaned her head back and looked up at the sky.

We sat there for a few minutes. She buried her feet in the pebbles beneath her swing. After a while, she got up and walked home.

The next day Bishop came to my door. He asked me out onto the lawn.

"I got something to show you," he said.

As soon as my feet touched the grass, he hit me a few times. It didn't hurt much, but I fell down and he left me that way.

Mom was gone when I got to her house. There was a note on the breakfast counter said she'd gone to work. I mulled through the refrigerator, but there wasn't much to eat. There were some light beers, so I had one of those and I decided to go look around town. I hadn't been home in a long time.

The first place I went was the mall. I guess I wanted to see somebody, but I didn't know who. I walked up and down the halls, but it was dead and I left.

I drove down to the water. I went to the same park where we had watched the butterflies. The bay was flat as a mirror, and there was fog, so it was hard to tell where the sky and water met.

Then I went up to the Service Building parking lot, but I couldn't see much. It didn't seem as high. I counted the seconds it took for spit to fall from my lips to the pavement below. One, two, three seconds.

I decided to go home and finish the rest of the beers, but on the way back I passed Gia's old street and I turned down it. I parked in front of her house. I didn't get out of the car. I stayed there listening to the radio softly. I wanted her to climb back out of her window. I wanted her to lead me back to the park. But, of course, she didn't.

I put my hand on my head. I lifted my hair. I ran my finger along the scar at the base of my widow's peak. I slipped my car into gear and drove down the road.

Gia wasn't the first girl Bishop had hit me over. The first time he hit me was in the sixth grade. He hit me with a broken broom stick that was used to bash a piñata at a Halloween party. He hit me because I kissed some brunette who was in our math class. She sat in the front of the class and Bishop and I sat in the back. I remember falling to my knees after the stick landed. There was blood on my face. My ears hissed.

Parents pulled the stick from his hand and forced him out the backyard, but later that night Bishop came to my window. He had me pull the bandage from my forehead so he could see the cut, and he promised it would never happen again.

I went back to my mother's house and opened another beer.

My phone rang. I didn't recognize the number. It was somebody from high school who I couldn't remember.

"How'd you get this number?"

"My wife works with your mom."

They asked about Bishop but I just hung up.

I decided to drive out to Port A where Bishop died. I had cooked at a small restaurant and bar there when I was younger. It was a tiny town, and I figured I could find the burnt down house easily.

I took the rest of the beer from my mom's refrigerator and wrote a note at the bottom of the one she wrote me. It said I'd be back in the evening.

I headed southeast toward the Island, then turned north and circled back around the bay. I got to Port Aransas and the roads were quiet. The fog was thick in the streets. The air was still. I drove around with my lights on. There aren't many neighborhoods. Most everything is condos and hotels.

It took me half an hour before I saw it. It was surrounded by yellow police tape, which sagged between thin wooden stakes. I got out of my car, stepped over the tape, and walked to the heap of ashes and skeletal posts that had withstood the fire. There was a neighbor across the street walking his dog.

"How long ago this burn down?" I asked.

"About a week tomorrow," he said.

"How'd it happen?"

"Bad wiring," he said. "All these houses are wired wrong. I've got an electrician coming out next week to look my house over so the same don't happen to me."

I walked over to the ashes and picked up a mound of soot. I let it crumble in my hand. It was dry and smooth. Black flecks fell through my fingers and floated down toward the ground.

I felt nauseous, staggered behind the garage. It was all that was left of the house. I wanted to be sick, but nothing came up. I just stood there, hunched over, with spit slipping from my lips and the muscles in my head constricting.

Once the urge passed I got into my car and drove over to the ferry to take it over to Aransas Pass. I got out of my car during the ride and looked down into the water. There was a massive school of giant redfish rolling gently near the surface. Their eyes looked tired.

"Shame isn't it," a man next to me said. He had on an orange sweater and a khaki hat with hooks in it.

"What's that?"

"That we can't just drop a net and pull 'em up."

"Why's that?"

"They're protected," he said. "Didn't you know that?"

"I'm not from here," I told him.

"Oh, boy. This school's been here for years, and them granola heads got together to outlaw fishin' 'em."

I shrugged, smiled and got back into my car. I stayed there

until the ferry docked.

I was hungry. I kept my eyes open for a restaurant as I drove.

There was a small white building with a sign that said "Family Diner."

I pulled over. There were only a few cars in the parking lot.

A bell rang as I opened the plate glass door, and a brown-haired girl looked up from a counter. "Just you?"

"Yes ma'am," I told her, and she picked up a red menu and told me to follow her.

She led me to a booth next to a wall that was covered in framed photographs. I looked at a few of them. There was one of a woman holding a baby on the beach, and she was surrounded by black butterflies.

"I remember that day."

"That's me," the girl said and pointed at the baby.

I smiled and took a seat at the booth. I ordered a Coca-Cola and a meat loaf sandwich. I stared at the pictures as I ate. Then I looked around at the pale yellow interior. There was a couple sharing a booth in the corner. They were pressed against each other and looking at a menu.

There was a woman at the register when I went to pay.

"You're the woman in the pictures," I said.

"Sure am," she said. "That's $5.41."

The register chimed and the cash drawer slid open. I reached for my wallet, and as I was handing her my money I noticed a Help Wanted sign that was taped to the front of the counter.

"Still looking for help," I said and nodded to the sign.

"Sure am. Know any cooks?"

"You're looking at one," I told her.

"When can you start?" she asked and laughed. I think she thought I was kidding.

"Right now."

Her smile faded. She nodded her head. Her eyes traced me over. She looked at my hands.

"Okay," she said. "Come with me."

She took me into the kitchen and introduced me to her husband. His name was Jim.

He was standing at the range sautéing some vegetables. He shot something from a squeeze bottle into the pan, and the liquid caught fire. I watched the flames as they danced across the pan, the blue fading into orange as the fire's fingers flickered.

Jim was talking, but I didn't really hear him.

"Well what do you think," Jim said and rubbed his hand down his shirt. "We could give it a trial run tonight just to see."

"Sure," I told him, but it was hard to look away from the fire. "Let me just run out and grab my knives."

I turned and walked out of the kitchen. I passed by the girl in the dining room. I tried to smile at her, but I'm sure it looked wrong.

The bell rang as I stepped from the front door, and when I heard it I knew that I'd drive off as soon as I got to my car. I couldn't help it. Something kept repeating. And I didn't want to think about what it felt like to burn.

STAMP #1

In Nuevo Progresso, at El Disco Super Center, they sell dozens of swords, none of them sharp, all of them beneath a sign that says, "Do not play with the swords." You really can't help yourself. Over the border, you can drink on the street. You walk up and down Benito Juarez Avenue sipping fruit drinks spiked with tequila, and the whole town is painted bright like light, and music floats in the air, and there are food trucks that perfume everything with the heavy smell of seared beef and fried bread. You're drunk by the time you get to the swords. You pick one up in your hand, feel its heft, slice the air. You can get anything there: shot glasses, pharmaceuticals, makeup, jewelry, crackers, chocolate, leather pants, baby bottles, guitars, handmade wooden furniture, bull whips, ceramic plates. But the swords draw the eye, pull you in, force you to break the rules.

"Pick one up," I say to my wife, holding my own sword, thumbing its dull edge.

She smiles, obliges, swipes a blade from the bundle and we clash as though at war.

In my left hand a Bohemia, in my right hand my sword. In her left hand a daiquiri, in her right hand a sword.

"Why are we fighting?" she asks as our blades strike again.

"Clearly," I tell her, "it's because you've disgraced my family name."

We strike blades again, and she dances back, her brown dress shimmies on her frame, her face boasts a proud smile.

"Well," she says, "your family is disgraceful."

"Blasphemy," I tell her, and once again our blades strike, chirping a metallic hiss that draws the attention of a thumb-shaped man with a whispery mustache who shakes his head at us and points to the sign. "No playing," he says. "Read sign."

I glance at the sign lazily. I nod but don't mean it. The man's name tag says, "Ernesto."

I smile. I set down my beer. "Ernesto," I say, and pitch him a thick-bladed sword from the clutch of them. "I hope you're ready to die."

THE DISHWASHER

The French asked Frijol to stay on late, intensity in his asking so Frijol knew what for—The French had killed another. The deaths and disposal had become more common, but The French paid good, paid cash, and Frijol had six children. Technically, he was a dishwasher, and, in his true hours, washing dishes was what he did. He kept the kitchen clean. He ruled the three sinks—his white shirt spotless, his hands soft from wash. But, when The French needed it, he'd do whatever so long as he was compensated.

Frijol grew up outside Monterrey in a broken little town amongst the bad mountains. His mother had an awful back and no teeth, and his father sold roasted corn to tourists at Cola de Caballo. Their home was made from cinder blocks and blankets. Their food was stewed over cardboard fires. Frijol came over in the hollowed-out seats of a Volkswagen

Beetle when he was fifteen. He didn't know English, so he shadow-lived the border. He told folks back home he worked in Chicago as a pimp and drug runner, but he'd spent his twelve American years checking classifieds for Spanish ads, cleaning shit and scrubbing dishes. When The French had him grind the first man, a tinge of pride came over him. It was a task he could brag to the back-home mountains over.

The French was not French, but he cooked that way. Frijol thought of him as The French or Chef, and the chef's wife had fake tits the size of a baby's head. She wore low cut blouses to showcase the tops of them, and, while The French was busy at the stovetop, jumping green beans in the hot pans Frijol would later scrub the oil from, she'd sit in the dining room with vanilla-eyed Mexicans who'd cross at Reynosa to eat and see the tops of her titties—her gently bent posture popping them further from her low-cut clothes. The French couldn't abide it, but he had a kind of fear of her.

"She's fucking them," he'd say to Frijol when he'd drop hot pans in Frijol's soapy water. Frijol wasn't certain of the meaning, but he had a good idea, and he'd pat The French's shoulder with compassion before plunging his hands after the deposited dish.

The French said nothing to her. She'd bring the Mexicans in to tour the kitchen, their hair slicked back with lavender oil and their eyes dyed blue with non-prescription contacts and their belts and pointy-toed shoes black leather, and the men would sort of bow at The French, as if to show admiration for his cooking, and then the wife would speak some magic-flavored words and she'd disappear out the back door with the international gents, a sort of money-scented silence about their movements and a sort of despicable fatigue in the body language of The French. Then, one day, The French brought in a meat grinder, and that was the same day Frijol was first asked to stay on late.

You must know that The French was not American, even though he was not French. Frijol had never heard of the country he came from, so he forgot the name of it the same way he'd forget English. But Frijol understood The French was a stranger on the border as Frijol was, and in that way Frijol considered The French a compatriot. So, when The French showed him the first body wrapped in black plastic, and the two fumbled it from the truck cabin and into the kitchen, and cut away the plastic to reveal its dead-blue nudity and the dark, cord-shaped stain of strangulation about the neck, Frijol felt a kind of duty to dispose of the thing, so the strange world the two men awkwardly lived in wouldn't spit them from its borders. It felt like the light of the kitchen would constrict as they sectioned the man into hunks the grinder could chew to bits.

Now you need to know how precious those tits were and how the wife would raise her eyebrows and encourage you to stare on at them, and how Frijol had looked at the wife's cleavage as though lost in hallucination, how the soft skin the color of childhood heaved forth a warmth that made your whole body throb like a banged finger, and while Frijol cleaved chunks of dead man from human skeleton and then broke the bones to bits with a hammer—so chunks of marrow splattered across the kitchen floor to be later washed down the floor drain with a hose—he thought how lucky the deceased to be for being able to see the wife in her naked entirety, because he had once seen what he thought was the color change of the start of her nipple as she rested her forearms against Frijol's sinks and encouraged him, with the slightest of smiles, to look at her, and how Frijol froze there as he looked and felt he was being born again against her breasts that were squeezed together so patiently by her clothing, so that the cleavage promised with the delicately folded flesh a finish, a grand finale unparalleled, and Frijol had no choice but to rush out to the dumpster once she'd left him and sit in a shadow feverishly jerking off in a constant fear of being caught—the damp stench of garbage painting the endeavor filthier. And, once he'd finished, once he came back in the kitchen, she came to him and smiled like she knew what he'd done, and this memory swirled through him as he ground the dead men, thinking of them as winners in the grand scheme of things. Always, they'd been strangled.

The day after the first man was fed through the grinder, the wife strutted through the kitchen checking her watch. The night pulsed on, and Frijol watched the back door, a constant fear that at any moment the door would open and they'd be dragged out by police, and the wife kept checking her watch. The French spoke to her. There was disappointment on her face. The French spoke to her again as she paced. She'd go to check the dining room, she'd come back and she'd pace. The French was mildly busy. He watched her as he tended the pans. They spoke again, and then the wife nodded. The French plated food for the customers. He spoke again to his wife. The orders died down. There were no tickets dangling in the window. Frijol was caught up with the dishes when The French walked by. The French laid a single finger on Frijol's shoulder, then placed that same finger to his lips as if to say,

"Silence," and he went to the walk-in.

What he made for her from her lover's flesh was not on the menu. The French only served his wife the human meat. Most of the man was sealed in vacuum packs and buried in the freezer, but, for whatever reason, The French would set aside enough of the ground man to feed to his wife on the following day. The first time he made her a hamburger. And, as if by some strange inclination, she ate it standing beside the grinder that had been used to produce it—the polished metal of the thing sort of shining at her as she chewed the man she checked her watch over. The French beamed as this occurred, and Frijol stood with an open mouth at the sight of it, as this birthed a new, incalculable curiosity in Frijol.

Frijol's name was not Frijol, he only called himself by the handle. Why did he do this? It was what his wife took to calling him for no reason other than she loved him and had bore his children and had fed him medicine when he was ill, brushing his black hair with the back of her hand as he stared at the ceiling wondering if he'd die. She was the only woman he'd ever slept with, even though, when he'd brag back home to the mountains, he'd tell strange stories of white women he'd been with in rented rooms.

But once he'd seen what The French had done, he couldn't help but think evil things as he stared at his wife. She'd be bathing their children, or folding their blankets, or dusting their furniture, or braiding her long, dark hair, and wrapping the end of the braid in a ribbon the color of sunset and he'd wonder as he watched her thin wrists and wide eyes how she'd taste dead, cooked and in his mouth, if he'd be able to detect if not told that he was eating the meat of his lover, because he'd seen the satisfaction on The French's wife's face as she'd devoured the men she'd been with, and he hoped there was something more human in him, and that he'd never be able to be drawn into the trick of eating a person he fucked while checking his watch for them.

"Well?" The French said. "Can you?"

Frijol nodded. Of course he'd stay. Of course he'd help. And, of course, The French would pay him.

WE ALL BECOME SOMETHING

The last woman I dated in any serious sense I had to quit because I hit her a few times and that's not the kind of person I am. I never hit her face. Her back and arms. Once where the neck meets the shoulder. Never while she looked at me. She learned that. Kept her face toward me and cornered when she'd see me near rage. We'd be in the stale light of an early morning, our minds clouded out with drinking, a sort of incident stench in the air, and she'd lean against the two walls of the breakfast nook with her eyes wide opened as I paced huffing breath till I calmed. I don't think she would have ever left me.

I packed my things late one night when this sick dream woke me. I dreamt my brother was still alive but badly burned and I dreamt he made more money than I did and was with the woman I'd beat. They'd dated for a while when he was living, and I always kind of knew that was why we lived together, and I figured it was why I'd hit her. I never hit a woman I'd been with before and I've not been with one long enough since to know if it's a thing I've become. When I hit her there was always this thing that'd happen right before. She'd look me over as though she wished me something better, as though my brother's ghost came alive inside her and she remembered some grander life lived.

The reason I left is because the dream reminded me how much I hated my brother. He had a temper toward me. He didn't always have it, but, when he was 13, he spent a summer with a boy named Brad whose older brother would beat on the two of them and torture them in ways. My brother told me once, while they were swimming in Brad's pool, the older brother came and shot birdshot at them, so they had to dive beneath the surface of the water where the shot's path would perish. He'd thump their ears. He'd pull their hair. He was six years older than either Brad or my brother—a man really— and there was nothing they could do. I suppose my brother took to thinking that was what being a brother meant. And while he never went as far as Brad's brother with his torturing, he'd do things like throw sand in my face and push me out of my skis during winter vacation, and I never forgave him for it, and, in some ways, I was glad when he died. I didn't want to live with a woman who'd smile when death took me.

So, I packed my clothes in a duffel, left a note and anything I had worth money, and I went and spent a few months in Port Aransas, Texas with a buddy who worked on a charter boat. My mother wired me money, and I picked up shifts on the boat cleaning fish, and I drank Mexican beers in a carpeted bar across the street from the Tarpon Inn where supposedly Hemingway used to stay when he came to fish Texas, but I am not a coastal person. I got sick of the island because you'd see everyone over and over again, and everyone wanted to be there too much, or didn't want to be there at all, and so we came up with a saying: Everyone in Port Aransas takes turns being the town drunk. And it was true, but I seemed to take too many turns, and there weren't enough new places or people, so after a while I got a reputation.

I took a job selling double wides to oil men in Victoria, Texas when the Eagle Ford Shale took off, and I'd walk fat-necked men through the show homes turning on faucets and flipping on lights and talking about carpet warranties and air condition tonnage. We advertised our homes by the pound, but prided ourselves on our products' amenities. To me, the houses seemed hollowed things. You felt a quake with every step you took, and you got the notion that you could dive through any wall like the Kool-Aid man, but I enjoyed my time there. My boss was a big shouldered Texas boy named Chet, and he was the displaced soul of a TV chef, and he liked to pecan-smoke briskets. He always had a pit going, and he'd offer up sandwiches to the folks who'd come to look at the homes we sold.

In the late spring while I was there he entered into a Bar-B-Q cook-off in Halletesville, Texas at an annual festival they have there called the Fiddlers' Frolic. I guess it was two things: It was a cook-off and fiddle competition. I knew some fiddle music, because I'd heard the bluegrass bands we'd bring through a bar called The Executive Surf Club in Corpus Christi where I worked as a teenager, and I knew Bar-B-Q, because I was Texas born and raised, and so my boss asked me along with him, though I'm certain he couldn't anticipate what happened. I saw the girl I used to beat.

It was terrible. I tried to play it calm, or to act as though I hadn't seen her, or to pretend as though I wasn't myself, or to seem as if I hadn't done what I'd done, but this heat just bit ahold of my face when she noticed me, and she had a new man aside her, and I could tell they had talked. Nothing's more hideous than people knowing you're worse than you'd like to be. I saw recognition in his face when he saw me, so I assume he'd seen a picture. He came to me. His pressed jeans clean as paper and his rattlesnake-skin belt near iridescent in the soft sun's light.

"I know you," he said and he spit in the dirt.

There was a heavy smell of smoke in the air, the lulled voices of crowd chatter, and, in the distance, I could make out the country-shaped music of some fiddle whining.

"That so?" I said.

"Is," he said, and he sort of popped his head around on his neck like someone shaking water out their ears. "And you know it," and he pointed to the old girl, "I hear you're a tough guy," he told me and sort of slapped at his chest, "you think you tougher than me," he asked, "you think you can take a boy that's rode rodeo his whole life? You think you can take a boy whose first meal was a pit bull steak? Whose father was a murderer and whose mother he never knew?" His eyes grew beady and he clenched his jaw. "Who the army couldn't handle? Who the law could not catch up with? Who the swamp could not contain? A boy raised catching crocodiles unaccompanied? A Louisiana outlaw with a Louisiana heart?"

My boss was tending to the pit just over my shoulder, and I suppose he heard the commotion and saw the mild crowd amassing to watch what might transpire between myself and this new man, because you can always tell when two men might hit each other, and he called over to me in his mild-Texas tone, "Everything alright?"

I looked at the big talker and looked back at my boss casually. "I'd assume so," I told him.

"Oh no, oh no," said the man, "it ain't alright for you by a long shot," and he put his finger up in my face so close I could see the cigarette stains on it, "you're about to feel the hurt of the century. You're about to wish your mother hadn't bore you, and that your father was a priest. You're about to swim in all the pain the world could know you. You'll wish you hadn't woke this morning, or if you had you'd woke a woman." Then he got all up near me. "Cause men don't hit women," he said. "Do they?"

I looked off at the girl I'd hit and she was sort of watching proudly, looking at me as if she'd gone and searched the earth for this hero who was about to throttle me in front of her so as to repair all the damages done.

"So how bout it fella?" the man asked, and by now the crowd around us was healthy and so quiet I could hear this lowing bluegrass dirge floating in from the competition, a slow note-pulled thing in the key of Appalachian sadness. Then the man asked, "You want some shit?"

I thought a moment. "Not really," I told him. "Shit's a bad thing to have." And then he sort of pushed me.

You ever seen that YouTube video "Afro Ninja"? I fisted the man twice in the face, the loud smack the only noise in the world, and he just went blank in his skull and staggered mildly like a drunkard pawing toward me as a baby may, until the girl came to grab him. "How can you live with yourself?" she told me, and she held her eyes wide at me in her old style, as if she thought I might strike her too if it wasn't something she'd done, and I looked back at my boss who seemed half aghast, half proud of me, but I didn't want to talk it over with him, and I went and got in my car and drove home, and I never went back to that job.

Here's what I kind of feel bad about: the new man and my old woman, they can't be happy together still. It's hard living with someone who's seen you get your ass kicked. I watched my father beat once. We'd just gotten ice cream, and when we were getting back in our car I opened my door too far and it clipped the car beside us—some sporty vehicle I can't reclaim the name of—and the man who owned it was sitting behind the wheel when it happened and he got out to inspect the damage and he began to yell in my window at me, and then he yelled at my father for allowing such a thing to transpire, but my dad just looked at him and said, "What the hell are you talking about?" I'm quite certain he was oblivious to the incident, but this man with his tight Polo shirt tucked into khaki shorts and his frosted-tip hair and Oakley sunglasses kept ranting about how I was a piece of shit because I'd dinged his car. My father was a man about my size—big enough to fight if provoked—and so he went to the car's owner with his fists clenched and told him he better pipe down. The man did not. He shoved my father and they took to fisting, but the man was tauter than my father and more spry, and my father hung with him for a minute or two, but then the man caught him with a good right and my father's nose bursted bloody, and I got out from the car then and hollered "Daddy," and that further distracted him, because he yelled at me, "Get back in the damn car," and while he was doing this the man landed a few more shots at his face, so I pulled the door closed and lay with my eyes shut and my fingers buried into my ears with my face smashed into the upholstery of the backseat until I heard my father's car door open. Then I heard a knock at my window and the man who my father'd fought was there grinning. "I just kicked your daddy's ass," he told me, and then my father drove us home quietly with tears kind of sitting in his eyes and his jaw clenched, and we never talked about that incident ever again, but I knew that we both thought about it whenever we were together, and somehow we had less of a relationship after that. He must have felt miserable over it, but it's a bit hard for me to truly know.

I don't have kids of my own. I have a niece who I watch from time to time—my sister's kid. She's a peach. I'd punch you in the face if you ever looked at her oddly, and when she's dating age I'll probably be the one who sits on the porch with the shotgun after midnight. Her father's whereabouts are unknown to me. A few weeks back I was watching her while her mom was at the doctor. My sister's fine, but she always thinks she's dying, and we live close enough to Houston that she can go get looked at by specialists every time she hears of some new ailment she might have. My niece and I were on the elevator going to the top floor because I figured there'd be a good view up there. We'd climbed aboard for no reason other than to waste time, and I let me niece press the number twenty and she grinned when the button lit. It was just us and another woman, and the woman thought my niece was cute and she smiled down at her.

"How old is she?" she asked, and I told her three.

"Three?" she said, and her tone struck me funny.

"Yes ma'am," I told her. "This last May."

"I don't believe it," she said, and my niece looked up at me with a drop of confusion in each eye, and then she held her three fingers out at the woman as if in support of me.

"Believe it," I said smiling, pointing down at my niece's three fingers, because really it was a brilliant gesture on her part.

"Huh," said the woman. "It's just that she's so small."

I looked down at my niece. At her blonde hair so soft you could sleep in it and at her eyes so blue they confused you. Her cheeks like prayers to Jesus. Her smile the reason Americans own guns. I clapped my hands at my niece, which is the signal that I want to hold her, and she jumped into my arms and I pulled her to my hip.

This dumb bitch. Did she not know? Could she not think?

My niece is healthy as hell, but we were in a twenty story building filled with doctors that other doctors had to send you to. People with magnetized machines who didn't even bother looking at your piss, because if you were so ailed to be in their presence it meant your cells or organs were not regular, and she stood on the elevator in the presence of my beautiful little girl telling my niece that she looked small for her age. She might've had the baby cancer. She could've had the children's AIDS. And this woman, with her velvet-red sweater and her skin the color of old cake icing was chucking out comments that might bring tears to my baby's eyes.

I forced it.

"Well," I said. "My niece, she's dying." And my niece looked at me with some suspicious appearance, but I just stared on at our new hideous friend.

She was supposed to go to the top floor with us. She was supposed to go all the way. I know that because the only button pushed was twenty, but I guess she got wise. I held my eyes on her like I was about to pull a knife and cut off her tits, but she just stared at the floor, sort of rocking back and forth, and I guess she wised up around the tenth floor, because she pressed twelve and got off in a weird panic, nervously smiling and saying, "Good day."

I kissed my niece when the door closed.

"You ain't never dying," I told her, and I shook my head at the then-closed elevator doors as we were drawn further skyward. I kissed my niece again, said, "And you ain't small for your age," I kissed my niece again, whispered, "it's just some folks are terrible," I kissed my niece again, whispered, "but not you and me."

Then the elevator doors opened and we got off. We found the window with the best view. "Everything looks tiny," my niece told me. Then we both pressed our faces against the glass.

BULLETS

Three of my friends lost their virginity to Daniele, and I bought a gun from her. The town we lived in was white-paper fresh, but we all had hoodlum blood. The best thing to do was walk the alleyways stealing small things from garages, or raiding ice chests for cold red wine, which we'd drink by the bayou while hunting crawdads we'd no intention of eating. The gun was cheap. The handle taped together. There was no clip for it, but Daniele gave me a handful of bullets. You'd have to load each individually. You couldn't kill a person with it, not that I wanted to. I wanted to take it to the old abandoned car dealership and shoot windows, but I didn't get the chance. One of my friend's mothers heard about my purchase and confiscated the pistol before I ever put it in play. It's probably for the best. I might have hurt myself.

A few weeks later Daniele asked me how I liked the gun. I shrugged my shoulders.

"Did you really sleep with Toby?" I asked.

"Yep."

"David?"

"Uh huh."

"Trey?"

She nodded.

"Why ain't you slept with me?" I asked.

"You didn't try soon enough," she said, "and I don't do that no more. I picked up Jesus. I won't do that again till I'm married."

"Since when?" I asked her.

"Since right before I sold you the gun."

Later on I was with Toby and we were wine drunk and ankle deep in bayou water.

"Was she any good?" I asked him.

"How should I know?" he said. "I've got nothing to compare it to."

I thought about Daniele a lot after that. Too much. I wrote her notes and begged and begged her to reconsider. To put down Jesus. To come around when my parents were out, but she never did.

I still had the bullets she sold me, but there was nothing I could do with them. I took a few in my pockets wherever I went. I'd touch them and think of her.

Eventually I lost those bullets. They probably fell out of my pockets, or I forgot them somewhere, or I threw them away, or I have them somewhere but just don't know.

To this day when I see a bullet I think of her.

I know this, she didn't make it till marriage. She got pregnant in high school, and she might have raised the kid, but I don't know what happened to her.

Last time I saw her, her belly was swollen up with that baby, and I shook my head at her, but I guess she didn't mind it.

"Still interested?" she asked.

I was surprised by that. I didn't think pregnant girls had sex. But apparently they do. Sometimes.

I've never owned another gun, and I haven't felt the need to shoot one.

I saw Toby recently, and I asked him if he remembered Daniele, but he just asked, "Daniele who?" I didn't press it. I guess if I could forget her I would too, but then I started wondering what it must have taken for Toby to lose her memory.

What we call a bullet today isn't really a bullet at all but rather a cartridge. It's got five parts, and they work like this: A casing-housed primer is struck, and it ignites gunpowder that sits in a shell, and this reaction launches a projectile toward a target, whatever that target may be. It always takes steps to get one thing to another.

I don't know how many steps it took me to get to Daniele or how many parts were involved in the process, but it'd be nice if you could step back and look at a schematic, because her memory serves no purpose, but somehow I tend to dwell on it, and I think I'd rather be like Toby. I think I'd rather move forward. Ignite. Launch on. And let her slip away soundless from the chamber of my mind.

SWEET DREAMS

Now I say, "Sweet dreams," because I'm tired of saying goodbye, because I don't think it works. I'll say "sweet dreams" in the morning, and I like it, because you can see the contemplation in people's faces, a sort of puzzlement, because they feel they've either misunderstood you, or that you've misused the language, and I feel (and I believe justly so) when people are confused is the only time they are truly aware they're alive, and so I'm doing strangers favors when I tell them "sweet dreams" when I see them in the coffee line. "Sweet dreams" as they stroll past me in the park. Is it crazy? Perhaps, but what isn't? And, when I took German in high school, and we learned the German salutations—Guten Tag, Guten Abend, Gute Nacht—and were told "never use Gute Nacht unless you are for certain that it is the last time you will see a person that day, or they are going to sleep," it occurred to me that the true equivalent in English is "sweet dreams." Really, it means so much. 1) It means your are going to sleep. 2) It means I don't want you to have nightmares.

It means more than those two things, but I'm not sure that language can say all the other things it implies. Have you ever drank milk from a mason jar? It means that. Have you ever worn a pair of jeans so long that they became as soft as the handshake of a child? It means that too.

There is a woman who I see every day and her name is Hilda and she is a hard blonde woman who I would like to be naked with, but she couldn't be naked with me, because it would be embarrassing for her, and I know that because when I tell her "sweet dreams" she bites her lip like it tastes bad, and she never says, "Only if I wake with you in the morning."

There is a man named Franklin who I see every day, and he is bald and he is thirty, and I tell him "sweet dreams," but maybe what I should really tell him is, "I'm sorry. I'm sorry that your hair fell out, and I'm sorry your parents named you Franklin, and I'm sorry that someone gave you the impression that you are important, because you're not, and I'm sorry that you look like a man in a city you don't know, looking for a car that you parked somewhere that you've forgotten the color of because it's a rental."

I'm sorry for lots of things. I have a daughter and I have a wife, but I'm not sorry that I have them, but I am sorry that they're sorry that they have me, and I'm sorry that my daughter hangs her head when I go to get her at school, and I'm sorry that when I tell her friends "sweet dreams" that she doesn't understand, and that she pulls me by the arm as the other children laugh at me, all of them with little cartoons drawn on their shoes and Anarchy signs on their backpacks. I should tell them, "When I was your age I drew Anarchy signs too." I should tell them that it's a waste of ink, that even there being a sign for the thing makes it impossible. I should tell the boys, "Be brave, kiss the girls." I should tell the girls, "Hold out for something better."

My wife has a girlfriend, and she thinks I don't know. Sometimes Lidia, her girlfriend, comes to the house and they sit in the front room and drink hot coffee and whisper about me, and I'll know they want their privacy, so I tell them "sweet dreams" and walk to the corner store to buy sunflower seeds and sit on the cement. I should tell them, "I don't mind that you love each other." I should tell them, "I think about your loving each other and it makes me feel alive."

They wouldn't even ask me, "Why do you feel alive?" If they did, I'd tell them, "Because it makes me confused. Because once upon a time I fell in love with my wife in autumn and we walked around holding hands and slow dancing when there wasn't even music, and that woman, the old wife, the wife I held hands with, would have blushed if she heard me telling strangers "sweet dreams," but she wouldn't have blushed a color to suggest, 'I can't believe you're doing this,' she would have blushed as if to say, 'I can't believe you're mine,' and that disbelief wouldn't have been built around the style of shame, it would have been built around the style of 'lucky me, oh lucky lucky me,' and she would have written my name a thousand times on a piece of paper that she'd carry always in her back pocket and kiss before she fell asleep at night.

Then there's the job. I don't have one, so my job is supposed to be finding a job, but I don't want one, so the job is to make my wife think I'm looking for a job and just not having any luck, which might be a harder job than actually finding a job, so I do things around the house. I take out the garbage. I change lightbulbs before they even burn out. "Sweet dreams," I say to the old lightbulbs as I spin them from their sockets. "Sweet dreams," I say to the new lightbulbs as I turn them on for the very first time. "Sweet dreams," I say to the garbage men who come to lug my trash can on their shoulders and heave its contents in the back of the truck, and then I watch my neighbors' garbage get added to my garbage, and I watch that garbage driven away.

It becomes our garbage. All of it. The whole world's. And I think it goes to the same place. And I think, when it gets there, it misses us. And I miss it too, but then, sometimes, I think, why even worry about it anyway. None of it was real. Or, if it was real, it was real in a way that would trick us. It's real in the way that says "sweet dreams" but really means "have a nice day, look both ways before you cross the street, make love with me Hilda, live hard while you're young, good luck finding that rental." But you can't just say those things, and life can't mean what it is.

It can't dance if there's no music. It's not going to smile just because it sees me.

ABOUT THE AUTHOR

Brian Allen Carr lives in the Rio Grande Valley of Texas. His short fiction has appeared in *Ninth Letter, Boulevard, McSweeney's Small Chair, Hobart* and other publications. His books include *The Last Horror Novel in the History of the World* (Lazy Fascist Press), *Motherfucking Sharks* (Lazy Fascist Press), *Short Bus* (Texas Review Press), *Edie and the Low-Hung Hands* (Small Doggies Press), and *Vampire Conditions* (Holler Presents).